THE HERO

by Edouard F. Coulon
illustrated by Shirley Beckes

Harcourt

SCHOOL PUBLISHERS

Printed in China

ISBN 10: 0-15-350451-X
ISBN 13: 978-0-15-350451-8

Ordering Options
ISBN 10: 0-15-350333-5 (Grade 3 Below-Level Collection)
ISBN 13: 978-0-15-350333-7 (Grade 3 Below-Level Collection)
ISBN 10: 0-15-357462-3 (package of 5)
ISBN 13: 978-0-15-357462-7 (package of 5)

2 3 4 5 6 7 8 9 10 985 12 11 10 09 08 07

Josh really loved baseball. The Stars were his favorite team. The player Ricky Callan was his hero. Josh had seen plenty of games on TV, but he had never been to a big league game. When he asked his father whether they could go, Josh's busy father always said, "Yes, when we get a chance."

One day, Josh's father came home with a big smile on his face. "My company gave me tickets to the game," he said.

"Wow!" shouted Josh. Maybe he could catch a foul ball. Maybe he could even get close to the players.

"The game is next week," Dad said.

It was hard for Josh to wait. He squirmed during an assembly in school, thinking about the game. Every night as he lay in bed, he tried to imagine the game. Sometimes he felt as if Saturday would never come.

Josh got up very early on Saturday. His father laughed to see that Josh was ready to go. He had on his blue hat, his team shirt, and he had his glove to catch a foul ball.

When they finished their pancakes, Josh's father said, "Time to go!"

They walked up the ramp into the stadium.
All the colors of the clothing in the stands
reminded Josh of the patchwork quilt on his
bed. The scoreboard flashed messages.
Josh bought a program and read every word.

At the game, Josh could see all the players at once. He could watch where every ball went. The crowd sounded louder, and the crack of the bat seemed sharper. The best part was when Ricky Callan hit a home run. The Stars won 7 to 4.

On the way to the car, Josh stopped. There was Ricky Callan in the parking lot!

"It would be great to have a program autographed by you," said Josh.

"Sorry, but I am in a big hurry," Ricky Callan said, and he just kept walking.

Josh was crushed. He said nothing as they drove home. Why couldn't Ricky Callan have been nice? Why did he just dismiss Josh? The day was ruined.

Josh said sadly, "I guess there aren't any real heroes."

"Maybe there are just different kinds of heroes," his father said as they pulled up to an apartment building.

"Where are we going?" Josh asked.

"You'll see," his father answered.

They met a woman named Mrs. Evans. She was glad to see them. "I used to have a job that was not very interesting. I also had a secret," Josh's father said.

"What was the secret?" Josh asked.

"I couldn't read," said Dad quietly.

"You couldn't read?" Josh asked.

"No, I couldn't. Mrs. Evans taught me to read in night school. Now she is my hero."

Mrs. Evans laughed. "Actually, your father is *my* hero because he worked so hard to learn."

Josh thought of all the things he could read. He could read newspapers, scoreboards, programs, and even street signs. Josh's father said, "I think a hero is someone who teaches you something important."

Josh thought for a moment. "Then I think I have two new heroes now."

Think Critically

1. How can you tell from the story that Josh loves baseball?

2. Why did being at the Stars stadium seem so different from watching a game on TV?

3. Why did Josh say he thought there weren't any real heroes?

4. Why did Josh say at the end of the story that he had two new heroes?

5. Who are your heroes? Why?

 Language Arts

Write About It Why do people want to get autographs from famous people? Write about whose autograph you'd most like to get and why.

School-Home Connection Ask friends or family members which sports teams are their favorites and why. Make a list of their choices. Look for things you might read about these teams.

Word Count: 521